Maisy Goes to the Bookshop

Lucy Cousins

WALKER BOOKS
AND SUBSIDIARIES
LONDON · BOSTON · SYDNEY · AUCKLAND

Today Maisy is going
to the bookshop.
She wants to buy
a new book.

We Love Books

Wow! The shelves are full of so many books!

Which one will Maisy like the most?

She reads a big brown book about bears …

One long blue book about fish …

a noisy
book about
trucks ...

Brrm,
brrm!

and a book about
things to draw and
paint. It's the best!

Ostrich, the shopkeeper, helps Maisy find a beautiful book about birds. She can't wait to read it with her friend Tallulah!

What a surprise! Charley jumps
out from behind the shelves.
"Ahoy, Maisy!" he says.

"I'm reading a book about pirates.
I can imagine **US** as pirates!"

Next they meet Cyril.
"One day I want to be a cowboy
or an astronaut! Look at this
amazing rocket!"

Hello Eddie!
What are you
reading about?

It's story time! Hooray! Ostrich reads a book about a dinosaur.

Then Maisy and friends share their favourite books.

Now everyone is feeling hungry.
The food at the café is so yummy!

Maisy pays for her books at the till and gets a receipt. "Thank you, Ostrich!" she says.

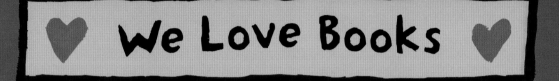

Bye Eddie! Bye Charley! Bye Cyril!
It's time for Maisy to get
the bus to Tallulah's house.

Maisy tells Tallulah about her wonderful day at the bookshop. She loves her present!

Then they read Tallulah's new book together. Over and over again ... and out LOUD!